Enid Blyton™

NODDY™

The Official Annual

This Noddy Annual belongs to:
Name
Address

Written by Caroline Brook. Designed and illustrated by County Studio.

Published by Grandreams Limited, 435-437 Edgware Road, Little Venice, London W2 1TH.

Printed in Belgium

£5.75

Contents

Hello, everybody.

It has been a very busy year in Toyland. I have had lots of fun with Big-Ears, the Tubby Bear family, Tessie Bear and all my other friends. In spring I had a very special surprise visitor, and in summer I had a very exciting time at a picnic on Farmer Straw's farm. In autumn Mr Plod had trouble with those naughty goblins, Sly and Gobbo, and in winter when it was snowing I gave Master Tubby Bear a real surprise! You can read all about my adventures in this annual. As well as stories, there are puzzles, a game, learning pages – and I'll show you how to make a hat just like mine! Have fun!

Love from

Noddy

Noddy's Special Visitor

It was spring in Toy Town, and Noddy had had a very busy time. He had cleaned his little House-for-One from top to bottom. He had brushed and polished and swept and washed, and now it was as clean and shiny as a new pin.

Noddy had cleared out his cupboards and drawers. He had filled a big box with things that he didn't need anymore. But he wasn't going to throw them away. There was a spring sale in town. Unwanted things were going to be sold to raise money for broken toys to be mended. Noddy was going to take his things to sell. He looked at the clock. "Good," said Noddy. "I will have time to deliver them before I have to pick up Mr Wobbly Man to take him to visit his cousin."

Noddy went outside and said hello to Master Tubby Bear, who had also been busy spring cleaning. He had been helping Mrs Tubby Bear, and was hanging out lots of washing so the spring sun could dry it.

Noddy had polished his little car until it was gleaming. He gave the bonnet a final rub, then jumped inside with the box of things on the seat beside him. "Goodbye!" said Noddy, and he waved to Master Tubby.

But something was wrong with Noddy's car! It would not go. Noddy heard a noise. It seemed to be coming from inside the car. Tweet, tweet! went the noise. Noddy frowned. That wasn't the kind of sound his little car usually made!

Noddy tried again, but the little car just would not go.

Along came Big-Ears on his bicycle. "Your little car looks extra clean and shiny this morning," said Big-Ears.

Noddy nodded his head. "Yes, it looks nice," he said. "But my little car won't work.

It's making the oddest noises, Big-Ears. It should go brum brum, but it's going tweet, tweet instead! Listen."

Big-Ears listened hard. Yes, Noddy's car was making a tweet, tweet noise.

Just then Bumpy Dog came along and started barking at the bonnet of Noddy's car. He was trying to tell them something! Noddy lifted up the bonnet and they heard the tweet, tweet noise again.

Bumpy Dog got up on his back legs and peered inside. "Look!" said Big-Ears, and he pointed inside at the engine.

Noddy looked. What a surprise! A blackbird had built her nest in his engine. She was sitting on it.

Noddy looked at Big-Ears. "What are we going to do?" he asked.

Big-Ears looked closely at the nest. "The blackbird has laid three little eggs in the nest," he said. "We mustn't disturb them. We can't move the nest until the birds have hatched out of the eggs and flown away." Noddy agreed.

"But what can I do?" he said. "I can't be a taxi driver if I haven't got a taxi car. I have an important job this morning. I have to take Mr

Wobbly Man to visit his cousin. And I have to take this jumble to the spring sale."

Big-Ears had an idea. "You'll have to use my bicycle as a taxi for the time being," he told Noddy. "You can carry your passengers in the little cart on the back."

Noddy wasn't sure. "I hope my passengers won't mind," he said. "The cart isn't as comfortable as my little car." But Noddy couldn't think of a better idea, so he jumped into the cart with his box of jumble and Big-Ears took him into town.

There was a table full of jumble in the town square. Noddy put his things with the rest. He looked at the things that were for sale. There was a big squashy red cushion. Noddy gave a sixpence for it, and put it in the cart. "Now my passengers will be more comfortable," he said.

Just then Mrs

Tubby Bear came along. She was pushing a little pram, the one she had used when Master Tubby was a baby. She didn't need it now, and was bringing it to the sale.

Noddy bought the pram for two sixpences. He and Big-Ears tied it to the little cart on the back of Big-Ears' bicycle.

"Now I can carry TWO passengers at once!" said Noddy.

Big-Ears and Noddy went off to collect Mr Wobbly Man. The pram came

in handy, because he had a very big suitcase!

Big-Ears and Noddy worked hard pedalling the bicycle all around Toy Town. People liked the new bicycle-taxi. Some of them thought it was more fun to ride in the little cart and the pram than in Noddy's car!

Each day, Noddy and Big-Ears looked at the nest in Noddy's car. First the eggs cracked open one by one, and baby birds hatched out. The mother bird was kept busy, bringing worms for them to eat. They grew a little bigger every day, and soon they all had feathers.

One morning Noddy got a big surprise. The nest was empty! The little blackbirds had gone! Noddy looked all around. There they were, sitting on Mrs Tubby Bear's washing line with the mother bird.

"Tweet, tweet!" they said, then flew away.

Noddy was pleased to have his little car back again, and he drove it to Toadstool House to show Big-Ears. Noddy had a bucket and a box on the seat beside him. "Thank you for all your help, Big-Ears," said Noddy. "Now, I've got a surprise for you."

Noddy gave his friend the big red squashy cushion to put on his favourite rocking chair. "And that's not all," said Noddy. "I'm going to give your bicycle an extra good clean and polish. It's my special way of saying thank you."

Mrs Tubby Bear asks, **"How much do you remember about the story?"**

- Who built a nest in Noddy's car?

- What colour was the big squashy cushion Noddy bought for sixpence?

- Who did Noddy and Big-Ears take to visit his cousin?

Answers: 1. A blackbird, 2. Red, 3. Mr Wobbly Man

Birds in the Garden

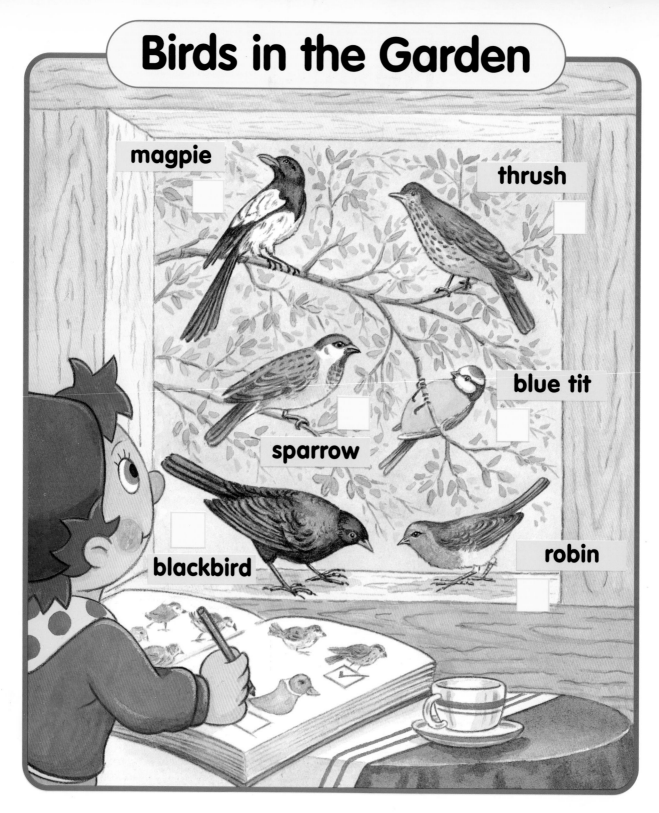

The bird that made its nest in Noddy's little car was a blackbird.

Noddy likes watching birds that come to his garden. Sometimes he puts out food for them. He has a little book with pictures in it, and the names of garden birds. Noddy ticks them off when he sees them.

You can do this, too. Put a tick in the little boxes when you see these birds in your garden, in a park or on wasteland.

Nesting

Here are four pictures of the mother blackbird on her nest. This time she has built her nest in a tree, not in Noddy's little car!

Can you put the pictures in the right order to tell the story?

Answer: The right order is c, a, d, b.

13

Eggs Everywhere!

The hens on Farmer Straw's farm lay lots of eggs. They lay them in some very odd places!

Noddy is helping Farmer Straw. He's collecting the eggs in his basket.

Can you help Noddy find six eggs on the page? Draw and colour an egg in the big basket each time you find one.

Noddy's House-for-One

This jigsaw puzzle shows a picture of Noddy's little House-for-One. But two of the jigsaw pieces are missing. Look at the jigsaw pieces at the bottom of the page. Which two will finish the jigsaw?

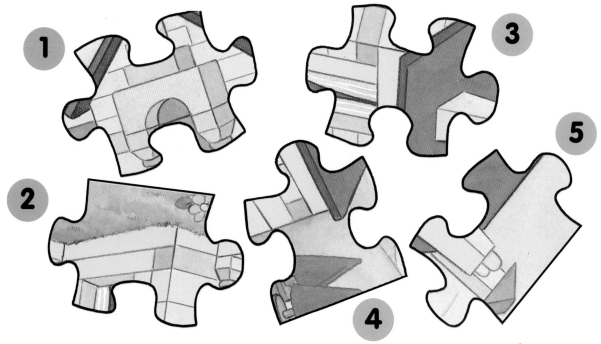

NODDY to the Rescue!

1. It was a spring day in Toy Town. The wind was blowing very hard.

2. Noddy was driving along in his little car when he saw Tessie Bear.

3. Tessie Bear was flying her kite. But she was having trouble.

4. The wind was so strong that it was hard for Tessie to hold on to the string.

5. Noddy stopped his car. He had an idea that would help Tessie Bear.

6. Noddy tied the kite string to his car. "Jump in!" he told Tessie.

7. Noddy drove along. Now Tessie could keep up with her kite.

8. "What a good idea," said Tessie Bear. "You are clever, Noddy!"

Flying Kites

Tessie Bear, Master Tubby Bear and Noddy are having fun flying their kites. But the wind has mixed up the strings. Can you sort them out?

1 Who has the blue kite?

2 Who has the red kite?

3 Who has the yellow kite?

Answer: Noddy has the red kite, Tessie Bear has the yellow kite and Master Tubby has the blue kite.

Up in the Clouds

Birds, bees, bats and butterflies can fly. So can machines like this toy aeroplane. Can you show Noddy the pilot the way to the airport through the maze of clouds?

Noddy Helps Out

One fine spring morning Noddy met his neighbour Mr Tubby Bear, who was standing outside his house looking at his watch. "Good morning, Mr Tubby Bear," said Noddy.

"Good morning, Noddy," said Mr Tubby Bear. "I'm waiting for the postman. He's late this morning."

Noddy drove into town in his little car. He passed Mr Jumbo's house and stopped to say hello. Mr Jumbo told Noddy that he was waiting for the postman too.

Noddy met Mr Plod in the town square. He had a big sack beside him, and he looked worried. "Is there anything wrong, Mr Plod?" asked Noddy.

"The postman has slipped and hurt his leg," Mr Plod told Noddy. "He won't be able to deliver the post today. And look," he said, pointing to the sack, "there's all this post to deliver. I don't know what to do. I can't take it because I have to direct the traffic."

Noddy looked at the big sack. He knew that Mr Tubby Bear and Mr Jumbo were waiting for letters. It was Big-Ears' birthday too. Noddy knew how disappointed his friend would be if he didn't get any birthday cards.

"I'll help you," said Noddy. "I'll deliver the post in my little car."

"Thank you very much, Noddy," said Mr Plod, and he loaded the sack into the seat of

Noddy's car.

Noddy was kept busy all day. Delivering the post was hard work.

Noddy took a parcel to Mr Sparks at the garage, and he had a holiday postcard for Miss Kitten. He had some letters for Bert Monkey and he had to drive all the way to Sammy Sailor's cottage to deliver a parcel to him. When he found a letter addressed to Mr Tubby Bear he hurried

home with it, because he knew Mr Tubby would still be waiting. Bumpy Dog barked to tell him that Noddy had come with his letter.

Everyone was grateful for Noddy's help.

Noddy saved Big-Ears' birthday cards until last, because there were lots and lots of them. He drove to Toadstool House.

When Big-Ears opened his front door Noddy

thought his friend looked a little bit sad.

"Happy birthday, Big-Ears," said Noddy. "I've got lots of birthday cards for you."

Big-Ears smiled. "Thank you, Noddy," he said. "I was beginning to think no one had remembered my birthday. The postman didn't bring me any cards at all."

Noddy told Big-Ears what had happened to the postman, and gave him the sack with his birthday cards in it. There was a big box addressed to Big-Ears, too, right at the bottom of the sack.

"Would you like to stay for a cup of tea after all your hard work, Noddy?" asked Big-Ears. Noddy nid-nid-nodded his head until the bell on his hat went jing-a-ling-a-ling. "Yes, please," he said.

While the kettle was boiling, Big-Ears unwrapped the big box. He opened the lid and lifted out a huge birthday cake with lots of candles on top.

"You have worked very hard today, and helped lots of people," said Big-Ears. "I think you deserve to have the first slice of my birthday cake. Well done, Noddy!"

Big-Ears' Birthday Cake

Noddy and Big-Ears enjoyed eating Big-Ears' birthday cake.

Here are two pictures of Noddy and Big-Ears. There are five things that have changed in the bottom picture. Can you spot the differences? Draw a ring around each one.

Noddy Sends a Postcard

Once, when Noddy was on holiday, he sent Big-Ears a picture postcard. He wrote his message on the back of the postcard. Then he wrote Big-Ears' address. An address is where someone lives.

Noddy stuck a postage stamp on the postcard to show that he had paid his sixpence to send it. He put the postcard into a postbox. A postman collected it with lots of other letters and cards. He sorted out the post, then put it in a post van and sent it to Toyland. The Toyland postman delivered the postcard to Big-Ears' house.

What is your name and address? Write it on the postcard above. Ask a grown-up to help you. Don't forget to draw a picture on the stamp!

The Picnic

It was summer in Toyland. The hot sun was shining and the sky was blue.

Noddy thought that it was too hot to work. "I'm going to take some time off," he said. "It's the perfect day for a picnic."

Noddy asked Big-Ears, Tessie Bear and the Tubby Bear family if they would like to come to the picnic with him. "We can all make different things to eat and drink, then share them," said Noddy. The others thought that was a very good idea.

Soon everything was ready. Four big picnic baskets stood outside Noddy's little House-for-One. Noddy put the baskets into his car and set off. "I'll meet you in Farmer Straw's field," Noddy told the others, who were going to walk there.

Noddy spread out a big rug on the grass under a shady tree at the top of a hill, above Farmer Straw's farm. The others soon arrived.

Noddy and his friends unpacked their picnic baskets. Big-Ears had made egg and cress sandwiches and a big jug of cold lemonade. Noddy had been busy too. He had put some little cubes of cheese on to sticks. He had made a big jug of cold lemonade too! Tessie Bear had made little buns with icing and cherries on top. She had made a jug of lemonade as well!

Next it was Mrs Tubby Bear's turn to unpack her picnic basket, the biggest of all. She had made a big chocolate cake, and some of Master Tubby's favourite chocolate cookies. And Mrs Tubby had also made, not just one, not two, but three big jugs of lemonade, one for each member of the Tubby Bear family!

Noddy laughed. "What a lot of lemonade! We won't be thirsty today, will we?"

The friends enjoyed their picnic.

They were playing a game of 'I Spy' when Tessie Bear pointed down the hill to the farm. "Look!" she said. "Black smoke!"

The others looked, and leapt to their feet.

"It's a fire!" said Big-Ears. "Come on, we'll go and see if we can help."

Noddy and the others found Farmer Straw and Mrs Straw near the big haystack. The dry hay had started to burn in the hot sun. "We are waiting for the firemen to arrive," Farmer Straw told them.

Master Tubby looked up at the thick smoke. He pointed, and said, "Look, up there!"

The others looked up. The farm cat had been asleep on top of the hay, and now he was stuck up there!

"Jump!" Farmer Straw told the cat, but he was too frightened.

Then Noddy had an idea. He ran back to the picnic field and came back carrying the big rug.

He held a corner himself and gave one corner each to Big-Ears, Mr Tubby and Mrs Tubby Bear. "Pull the blanket towards you so that it stretches out tight," said Noddy. The blanket made a kind of flat platform.

Noddy called up to the cat. "You can jump now," he said. "You'll be safe. We'll catch you in the blanket."

This time the cat jumped, and he landed safely on the soft blanket that Noddy and his friends were holding.

Just then the firemen arrived,
ringing the big bell on the fire engine. They
soon put their tall ladders against the
haystack and climbed up. They
squirted water through hoses,
and very soon the fire
was out.

It was very hot work for the
firemen in their safety helmets
and thick uniforms, and when
they had finished they felt
very thirsty.

"We've got just the thing
for you!" said Noddy, and
he and Master Tubby and

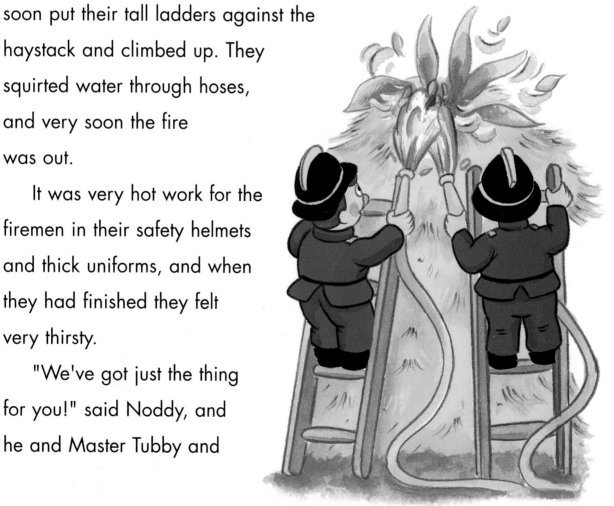

Tessie Bear ran back to the picnic field again.

They came back carrying the big jugs of cold lemonade. Noddy was right – a cold drink was just what the firemen needed! "Thank you, Noddy," said the firemen.

Noddy and his friends and Farmer Straw and his wife enjoyed the cold lemonade too.

The only one who didn't like the lemonade was the farm cat. So Mrs Straw gave him a saucer of milk instead!

Fire Safety

"Fires and the smoke they make are very dangerous. There are three important ways to stay safe. Try to learn and remember these rules if there is a fire."

1 **GET OUT.** Leave the house at once. Close doors behind you.

2 **STAY OUT.** Never go back into the house for anything.

3 **CALL OUT THE FIRE SERVICE.** You can do this by telephoning 999.

• Fire engines have big tanks of water. The water is pumped out through hoses. Firemen point the hoses at the fire to put the flames out.

• Fire engines have long ladders, too. Firemen sometimes have to climb up them to rescue people from high buildings.

Noddy says, **"Firemen are specially trained to put out fires safely. You must NEVER try to fight a fire yourself. Leave it to the experts."**

Lemonade

"My friends all made real lemonade for the picnic. I'll show you how to make it. It's easy, and it tastes much better than the fizzy sort you can buy in the shops. Remember, kitchens can be dangerous places. Always ask a grown-up to help you."

You will need: 3 lemons, 400g sugar, 500ml boiling water.

WARNING!
Note to parents: You must always help and supervise your child in the kitchen.

1 Squeeze all the juice from the lemons.

2 Put the lemon juice and sugar into a plastic jug.

3 Ask a grown-up to add the water to the jug. Stir with a spoon until the sugar has melted.

4 Put the jug into the fridge until the lemonade is very cold. You can add ice cubes if you like.

33

The Apple Orchard

1. One day Noddy and Big-Ears went to visit Farmer Straw's farm.

2. Farms are busy places. Noddy and Big-Ears like helping by doing jobs.

3. It was the end of summer, and the trees in the orchard were full of apples.

4. Noddy and Big-Ears helped pick them. They put the apples in baskets.

5. Soon they had filled all the baskets. But there were still some apples to pick.

6. "Where can we put the other apples?" said Big-Ears. "The baskets are full."

7. Noddy had an idea. "I know where to put them!" he said.

8. Noddy and Big-Ears put the rest of the apples in their hats! Clever Noddy!

On the Farm

There are lots of things to see on Farmer Straw's busy farm. Count the different animals, then write the numbers in the little boxes.

pig ☐

sheep ☐

cow ☐

dog ☐

hen ☐

duck ☐

cat ☐

goat ☐

Sports Day

Every summer Miss Prim organizes a special sports day at the Toy Town school. It's not just for the pupils. Everyone in Toyland comes along to join in the fun.

This year Miss Prim asked Mr Plod to do a very special job. She asked him to start all the races by blowing his police whistle. She asked Big-Ears if he would help too. He had a very important job to do. He was going to be the judge.

The egg-and-spoon race was the first event. Noddy and the other runners all held a spoon with an egg balanced on it. They stood in a line and waited until Mr Plod blew his whistle, then they set off.

Noddy ran as fast as he could. His head went nid-nid-nodding and his little bell jingled as he ran. But Noddy ran so fast that his egg wobbled off his spoon and broke on the ground. Poor Noddy!

Sammy Sailor and Tessie Bear dropped their eggs too. Mr Wobbly Man wobbled this way, then he wobbled that way. Every time he wobbled it looked as if his egg would wobble off his spoon, but then he wobbled the other way again – and kept it on. Clever Mr Wobbly Man!

Soon all the eggs were broken. All except Mr Wobbly Man's. He wobbled across the finishing line. "Mr Wobbly is the winner of the first race," said Big-Ears, and Miss Prim gave him his prize – a hard chocolate egg that would not break, even if he dropped it!

The running race was next. Mr Plod blew his whistle and the runners set off. The runners had to run for as long as they could. The one who kept running longest would be the winner.

Noddy's little legs went fast for the first three times around the track, but then he got tired. So did Sally Skittle and Sammy Sailor. So did all the other runners. But Clockwork Mouse and Clockwork Clown had wound up their keys as much as they could, and they ran on...and on...and on....

When Mr Plod started the sack race Clockwork Mouse and Clockwork Clown were still running around the track!

The runners in the sack race had to jump along with their legs inside a sack. It was very tricky! Master Tubby Bear likes jumping.

He had practised at home, using one of Mrs Tubby Bear's old pillowcases for a sack, and he won the race easily. He was pleased with his prize.

Can you guess who won the strong man contest to see who could lift the biggest weight? Yes, it was Mr Jumbo. He pinned the rosette Miss Prim gave him on to his head dress.

There was one more race to run. "The last race is the three-legged race," said Mr Plod. "Please line up with your partners." Tessie Bear ran up to Noddy. "Will you be my partner, Noddy?" she asked.

Noddy was
pleased. "Of course I will!" he said.

There were a lot of runners in the race. Mr Plod tied
Noddy's left leg to Tessie Bear's right leg. Noddy put his arm around
Tessie, and Tessie put her arm around Noddy. They had to run together,
using three legs, not four!

As soon as they heard Mr Plod's whistle, Noddy and Tessie Bear set
off as fast as they could. Noddy's head went nid-nid-nodding, and the
little bell on the end of his hat rang ting-a-ling-a-ling.

Noddy and Tessie Bear passed Sammy Sailor and Master Tubby Bear.
Then they passed Martha Monkey and Bert Monkey. Noddy and Tessie
ran so fast that Noddy's hat came off, ting-a-ling, and so did Tessie's
bonnet. But they didn't stop to pick them up, and they won the race!

Noddy and Tessie Bear got special prizes – little stools with three legs
that Big-Ears had made!

After the races everyone had tea and cakes in the big tent. Noddy
and Tessie sat on their little three-legged stools to eat.

Noddy and all the others were leaving to go home when Noddy heard a crickle-crackle sort of noise. Can you guess what it was? Yes, Clockwork Mouse and Clockwork Clown were still running around the track!

Miss Prim asks, **"What do you remember about the story?"**

• Who blew his whistle to start the races?

• Who won the egg-and-spoon race?

• Who was Noddy's partner for the three-legged race?

• What was Master Tubby Bear's prize for winning the sack race? Join the dots to find out!

Answers: 1. Mr Plod, 2. Mr Wobbly Man, 3. Tessie Bear

start

The R
Race

1 2 3 4 5 6 7 8 9 10 11 1

44

30 **29** **28** **27** **26** **25** **24** **23** **22** **21** **20** **19** **18** **17** **16** **15** **14** **13**

finish

You can play the Running Race Game with a friend. One of you can be Clockwork Mouse. The other can be Clockwork Clown.

You need a counter each, and a die. Take turns to roll the die. If you roll 1, move your counter 1 space along the running track. If you roll 2, move your counter 2 spaces, and so on. The first one to get to the finishing line is the winner!

unning Game

Make a Hat Like Noddy's

"Do you like my little blue hat with a bell on top that goes jing-a-ling-a-ling when my head goes nid-nid-nodding? I'll show you how to make a hat just like mine. Ask a grown-up to help you."

You will need:
- blue card
- yellow card
- safety scissors
- double-sided sticky tape
- non-toxic glue

1 Cut out a triangle of blue card. The base should measure 40cm. The sides should both measure 30cm.

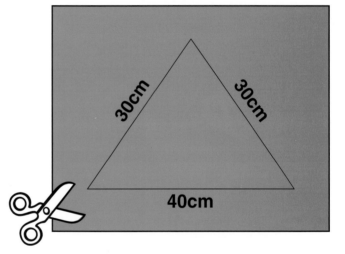

30cm   30cm
40cm

2 Stick a strip of double-sided sticky tape down one side of the triangle. Press the other side on top so that you make a cone shape. Trim the base to make a neat edge. The picture shows you how.

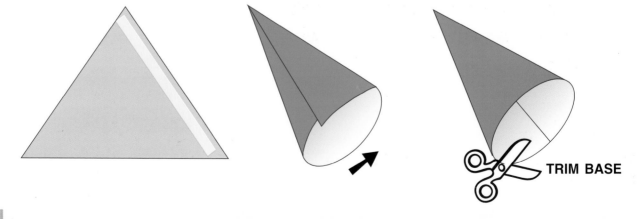

TRIM BASE

46

3 Cut out two circles of yellow card. They should measure 5cm across.

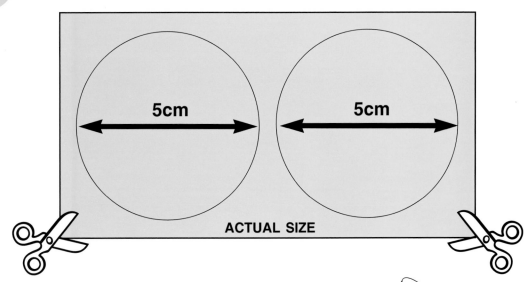

5cm   5cm

ACTUAL SIZE

4 Put some glue on the back of one circle. Press the circles together back to back, with the point of the hat in between. Press firmly.

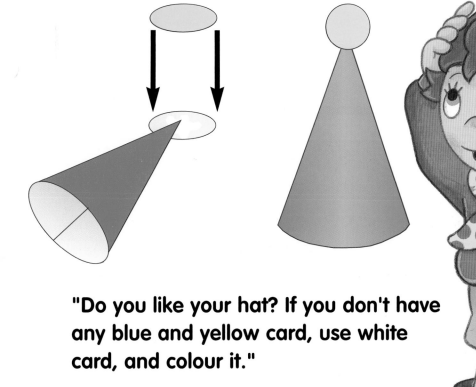

GLUE

"Do you like your hat? If you don't have any blue and yellow card, use white card, and colour it."

Warning to parents:

You must always supervise your child when using glue and safety scissors.

The Big Mushroom

1. It was autumn in Toyland. Cold winds blew. Leaves fell from the trees.

2. Noddy had been busy all morning collecting mushrooms in Dark Wood.

3. Noddy was on his way home when it started to rain. He hurried along.

4. Noddy met Clockwork Mouse. "Oh, Noddy, I must get home!" she cried.

5. "I'm afraid the rain will get into my clockwork and damage it," she said.

6. Noddy decided he would help her. But how? Then he had a good idea.

7. Noddy gave Clockwork Mouse the biggest mushroom from his basket.

8. "Hold it over your head like an umbrella to keep dry!" said Noddy.

Gold Buttons

It was autumn in Toy Town. The weather was getting colder. The leaves on the trees turned from green to brown and fell to the ground. They made a scrunchy carpet.

One morning the wind was blowing very hard. It swirled the dry leaves up into the air. It was Mr Plod's day off. He had lots of jobs to do. One of them was to sweep up all the leaves outside the police station.

When Noddy drove past the police station, on his way back from taking Mr Jumbo to visit his friend, he stopped to say hello.

Mr Plod looked different without his smart policeman's uniform on. He had washed it and was hanging his jacket on the washing line. The strong winds would soon dry it. "Your uniform looks very smart," said Noddy.

Mr Plod nodded his head in agreement. "Yes, it does, doesn't it?" he said. "And it will look even smarter when I've polished the badge on my helmet and the buttons on my jacket. The

50

buttons will look like ... GOLD!"

Now just at that moment, who should be passing by but those naughty goblins, Sly and Gobbo. They didn't want Mr Plod to see them, in case he took them into the police station to ask them questions about naughty things they had done, so they crept past, hidden by some bushes. When they heard the word GOLD they stopped to listen. But Mr Plod didn't say anything else except, "Goodbye, Noddy!"

"Did you hear that?" Sly whispered to Gobbo. "Buttons made of GOLD!"

Sly and Gobbo waited until Mr Plod had gone back into the police station, then they peered over the fence. Gobbo pointed. "Look, over there," he said. "On the washing line. Mr Plod's jacket has GOLD buttons!"

"Gold!" said Sly. "What are we waiting for? Come on!"

A little while later Mr Plod went outside to take his jacket off

the line. The wind had blown it dry. He had already polished the badge on his helmet until it was bright and shiny. Now he sat down to polish his buttons to match. But all his buttons were gone! There was not a single button left on his jacket!

When Noddy drove by in his little car again to collect Mr Jumbo, Mr Plod waved at him. "Stop, Noddy, stop!" he called.

Mr Plod told Noddy what had happened. "Now who can have taken

the buttons off my uniform?" asked Mr Plod.
"It's a mystery."

Noddy had an idea. "I saw
Sly and Gobbo in the bushes
near the police station this
morning," he told Mr Plod.
"Do you think they might have taken your buttons?"

"Aha!" said Mr Plod. "I think you might be right, Noddy. Come on.
Let's go to Dark Wood and find out."

Noddy and Mr Plod soon found Sly and Gobbo. "Did you take my
gold buttons?" asked Mr Plod.

Sly and Gobbo shook their heads from side to side. "No, we didn't
take them," said Sly.

"But we know who did!" added Gobbo. "We saw some black and
white birds sitting on the washing line. Magpies. You know how much
magpies like shiny things, don't
you? They take them back to their
nests."

Mr Plod knew all about magpies
and their liking for shiny things.
"The magpies must
have pecked
off my shiny
buttons,"
he said.
"Let's go
and find them, Noddy."

Mr Plod thanked Sly and Gobbo for their help. The goblins just smiled. Noddy wondered why Sly and Gobbo were being so helpful. It wasn't like them at all.

"The nest is in the big oak tree," Sly told Mr Plod. "Right at the top."

Mr Plod and Noddy borrowed Big-Ears' tall ladder. They asked Big-Ears if he would help by holding the ladder steady while Mr Plod climbed up. It was a long climb, and Mr Plod had to be very careful that he didn't fall.

The autumn light faded, and soon it was getting dark in Dark Wood. Noddy was wandering around as he waited, kicking the scrunchy dry leaves, when something caught his eye. He looked into a deep, dark hollow at the base of a tree. Yes!

There was something shiny inside. Noddy put his hand into the hole and felt something round and hard.

"OUCH! GET OFF!" came a voice from inside. Noddy pulled hard and out came, not a button, but Sly the goblin! Noddy was holding his long nose!

Out came Gobbo too. Noddy thought
that they looked as if they had done
something naughty.

Noddy reached inside
again. He felt something round
and hard again. This time it was
one of Mr Plod's buttons! Sly and
Gobbo had taken the

buttons and blamed the magpies. They had
hidden them in the tree hollow and were
going to sneak away with them later.

Mr Plod lead Sly away by the
collar. He made Sly and Gobbo
carry Big-Ears' ladder back to Toadstool
House, then he took them to the police station.

"Are you going to lock them up?" asked Noddy.

Mr Plod shook his head. "No, I've got a special job for these two
naughty goblins," he said.
"They are going
to polish my buttons
until they gleam, and
then they're going to
sew them back on to
my uniform. That will
teach them a lesson!"

A Story to Read

Noddy told Master Tubby Bear all about Sly and Gobbo and the gold buttons when he got home. Can you read the story? The pictures will help you.

1. (   ) hung his (   ) on the (   ) to dry. When he came back the gold (   ) had gone! Who took them?

2. (   ) came along in his little (   ). He had seen (   ) and (   ) near the (   ). They were hiding in a (   ).

3. Sly and Gobbo said some (   ) had taken the buttons.

Here are the words that match the pictures:
Mr Plod, jacket, washing line, buttons, Noddy, car, Sly, Gobbo,

56

4. Mr Plod got Big-Ears' tall (   ) so he could look in their (   ). (   ) held the ladder.

5. Noddy waited. He kicked the (   ). He saw something shiny inside a hole in a (   ).

6. He pulled out Sly by the (   ). Out came Gobbo too.

7. Then Noddy pulled out Mr Plod's gold buttons. Naughty goblins!

police station, bush, birds, ladder, nest, Big-Ears, leaves, tree, nose

Snow Noddy

It was winter in Toy Town. One afternoon, Noddy was putting coal on the fire when he heard a 'thud' on the front door of his little House-for-One.

He opened the door to find out what it was. There was snow stuck to his door. Noddy had to duck his head down as a

big snowball came flying towards him. It just missed him.

Outside, Master Tubby Bear was laughing. He had thrown the snowballs at Noddy's front door.

"The snowballs were just a little surprise for you, Noddy," said Master Tubby Bear.

"Naughty Tubby Bear!" said Noddy.

When Noddy went out a little later he sat on the seat of his car, then jumped up again. Someone had put a snowball on his seat. The snowball had melted and now the seat – and Noddy's trousers – were all wet.

It was naughty Master Tubby Bear again. "That's another little surprise for you, Noddy," he said.

"You are naughty, Master Tubby Bear!" said Noddy.

Just then, Tessie Bear arrived. She had come to have tea with Noddy. Tessie and Noddy

watched Master Tubby Bear from Noddy's window. He spent a lot of time building a big snowman.

When Mrs Tubby Bear called Master Tubby in for his tea, Noddy and Tessie got busy.

They put on warm scarves and mittens and went outside.

Noddy stood beside the snowman Master Tubby Bear had made. Tessie Bear covered him in snow. She patted and smoothed the snow until Noddy was completely covered. All that could be seen of him was the little bell at the end of his hat.

Tessie Bear hid behind a bush to see what would happen.

When Master Tubby came out again he was very surprised to see the new snowman.

And how he jumped when the Snow Noddy tapped him on the shoulder and nid-nid-nodded his head so that

the bell on his hat went jing-a-ling-a-ling!

Noddy jumped forward, shook himself hard, and all the snow fell off him. Some of the snow landed on Master Tubby Bear.

"That was my little surprise for you, Master Tubby Bear!" said Noddy.

Goodbye!
See you next year!